false start

piper rayne

Cover Design: By Hang Le

1st Line Editor: Joy Editing

2nd Line Editor: My Brother's Editor

Proofreader: My Brother's Editor

FALSE Start

about false start

The start of Lee Burrows and I was a college girls' biggest fantasy.

Campus' most popular guy, the starting quarterback, the same guy I've crushed on forever, notices me—the quiet introvert.

Although, he never would've noticed me if he didn't need my help passing our biology class. I didn't think I had a chance with him until he started flirting with me and asking me questions like, "Who was the guy you were talking to?" and "Do you have a boyfriend?"

It took a few tutoring sessions before we ditched the library to "study" at Lee's apartment.

It was a fantasy come true until I found out the truth and vowed that Lee Burrows would *never* get another chance with me again.

one

. . .

Lee

I WALK toward the stadium instead of driving across campus because my truck is out of commission. Talk about a shitty twenty-four hours. First, I get a call yesterday from the mechanic that my truck repair is a thousand dollars, which I don't have, and then Coach Buxby called to tell me he wants to see me before my first class this morning. For what? I have no idea. This is the one morning out of the week that we don't have an early morning workout, and I would've chewed off my left arm for an extra hour of sleep, but no one tells Coach no.

Our team is killing it this season. Correction: I'm killing it. Sure, the team is playing well, but it's my arm and my eye as the quarterback that's really making the difference. Hence why I'm here on a full ride scholarship. My first two years playing for the Wolverines were good, but this year is shaping up to be even better.

So, I know Coach doesn't want to see me because of my performance on the field.

I nod and say hello to the people I know and smile at the

ones I don't, because even if I don't know them, they know me. It's part of being the starting quarterback at a Division One college.

We're already a month into football season. October in Michigan usually means you're freezing or you're sweating, and it changes every year. One year we could have snow and the next it's in the seventies three out of the four weeks. But right now, it's the perfect fall day that people in the Midwest brag about. There's a slight chill, but my sweatshirt keeps me warm enough. The leaves changing colors into golden yellow, auburn, and orange reminds me of home. British Columbia, Canada, is beautiful in autumn, and a piece of me always yearns to end up back there, even if not all my childhood memories are happy.

I go inside the stadium, giving a nod to Horace, the security guy, and head straight down the hall to Coach's office. The door is open and he's sitting behind his desk with the paper open, a danish and coffee next to him.

I peek my head in. "Morning, Coach."

He waves me in. "Burrows, have a seat."

I sit in one of the two chairs across from his desk and lean back. The room is silent. He nods and steeples his fingers, studying me with a stern expression.

Coach Buxby couldn't be more opposite than most D1 coaches. He's in his late fifties with greying hair at his temples and a perpetually unshaven face. It's not a beard exactly, more like he just didn't shave for a few days in a row. His protruding belly makes me think of a small town high school coach rather than a D1.

Ever since Coach recruited me, we've gotten along. Which is why his pissed off expression makes the muscles in my jaw tense.

He's still yet to say anything, and I rack my brain for any reason why he'd want to see me. I finally say, "So... what's going on? Why'd you need to see me?"

He sighs. "Spoke to your biology professor yesterday."

I roll my eyes. Fucking Professor Sherman. The man is a complete dick who doesn't understand the pressure of being a college football player. Then again, it doesn't help that he's more of a chess fan than football. "It's not my strongest class."

"He says you're failing." The line between his eyebrows deepens into cavern-like levels.

"It's a D and there's a test next week. I do good on that and we're golden."

I suck at all science, especially biology for some reason. I'm holding a B average GPA. Regardless, I should've figured out this was the reason Coach wanted to see me, but I thought I had time to bring my grade up.

"I don't have to remind you that if you don't turn the grade around, you'll be suspended until you get it up."

My hands clench into fists. "I have time, Coach. The grade isn't final."

He holds up his hand. "You know the rules. If at any time, your grades aren't all Cs or better, you're suspended."

"Coach… you can't seriously suspend me because I'm pulling a D in biology?"

He leans in over the desk. "Never said I wanted to, Burrows. Rules are rules and you don't get a pass no matter who you are. And what would you do if you go out in that game on Sunday and get injured? What would your future look like? It's why my rules are clear. You earn your education while playing football. End of discussion." He picks up his coffee and takes a sip.

The entire time Coach is talking, all I can see are my dreams of playing professional football going up in smoke. What the hell would I do with myself if I couldn't play football for a living?

My hands wrap around the arms of the chair, tightening until my knuckles are white. "That can't happen."

"Then you need to get your act together and improve your grade."

Easier said than done. I may not have put my best effort into that class, but I have been trying. It's too late to drop the class, plus I need it for my graduation credits. So even if I got out of it this semester, I'm taking it at some point in the future.

"The team needs me," I say as one last ditch effort to see if he can make this all go away.

He sighs and stares at me for a long moment. His hands fist on his desk. "You don't think I fucking know that? But I'm not bending the rules for you, Burrows. Even if losing you puts us at a disadvantage."

I straighten up, hands held up in front of me. "What can I do?"

"Professor Sherman must be feeling nice, because he's setting you up with someone from your class to tutor you for the next month. There's an assignment and a test within that time period that you need to pass. Then you'll be able to stay on the team as we roll into the playoffs."

I nod as frantically as my heart beats. "I can do that."

"Good." He leans back and sips his coffee again, then takes a bite of his danish. A little crumble rests in his beard. "I'll be keeping up with Professor Sherman. Now get the hell outta here."

"Thanks, Coach." Without a word, I grab the strap of my backpack and hoist it onto my shoulder, then turn and make my way to the door.

"And Lee?"

I stop and turn to face him.

"You need to take this seriously. The university won't hesitate to remove you from the team if necessary."

My stomach turns over. "I got this."

And I mean it. I didn't become a D1 quarterback because I don't know how to set a goal, then work hard to accomplish it. No, I'm going to do whatever it takes to pass this class and not miss one single game. The last thing I need is pro teams thinking I'm a problem because that's when you slip in the draft.

———

On my walk across campus, all I can think about is what will happen if I can't get my grade up in biology. The entire future I've envisioned my whole life could disappear.

My phone buzzes in my back pocket and I pull it out and see my older brother Kane's name on the screen. The guy has always had a sixth sense for when shit is going on with me. All part and parcel of him basically filling a parental role for me after my dad died and my mom couldn't claw her way out of her grief.

I send the call to voicemail, not wanting the lecture from him right now, although at some point I'll have to ask for another loan to get my truck from the mechanic. One problem at a time.

Kane's living his best life right now. At almost twenty-seven, he's been playing professional hockey for years and is one of the best goalies in the league. I'd probably feel pressure to live up to my big brother's accomplishments if I came from any kind of normal family situation, but my mom doesn't really praise either one of us on our accolades.

Still, I don't want to tell him that I've put myself in a situation that threatens my place on the team. Not yet anyway. Not until I have the situation under control.

I arrive at the Biological Sciences Building and head into my auditorium.

Professor Sherman is preparing his lecture and doesn't seem to sense me eyeballing him as I make my way to my seat. My shitty grade isn't his fault, but he ratted me out. I've had teammates failing classes and the professor goes to them before Coach. Gives them extra assignments to complete to boost their grade.

None of my teammates are in this class, so I take my usual spot in the last row and plop my backpack down in the empty seat next to me. The rest of the class trails in as I bury my head in my phone. Then I hear Professor Sherman call a girl over. They chat for a minute and both glance at me.

I'm guessing she's my fucking tutor.

I've never noticed her before. Then again, she sits in the front row. She wears dark-rimmed glasses, and her long dark-blonde hair is pulled into a ponytail. Her clothes don't show off her assets. It's almost as if this girl does everything in her power not to let the opposite sex know she's a woman.

Whatever. I don't care who the professor gets to tutor me as long as they're smart enough to teach me so I can pass.

two

· · ·

Shayna

NORMALLY I WOULD BE TYPING my notes into my laptop at seventy words per minute, but my concentration is only on one thing this entire biology class—Lee Burrows.

Not that I can see him. He always sits at the very back of class, whereas I'm always in the front row. And even though his presence always practically suffocates me, today it's even worse because Professor Sherman asked me to tutor Lee.

Still, this is Lee Burrows. The starting quarterback for the football team. The "it" man on campus.

He's a legend around here.

Whether you're a fan of college football like me, or only into the fact there's no doubt he'll be drafted, you love him. Girls all giggle and stalk him with their eyes when he walks past. Or they just strategically put themselves in his path for him to notice them.

I'd love to say I'm above it all, but the truth is, I admire him too. I just do it from afar.

And now I'm going to spend a few nights a week with

him, alone. He better put forth the effort he needs to pass this class.

Fear cripples me, because any time I'm around a guy who's even remotely good-looking, I inevitably end up stammering and going pink-cheeked.

I shake my head. None of those problems matter right now. I need to pay attention to Professor Sherman because he's already wrapping up the lecture. He assigns our reading assignment, and the quiet lecture hall turns chaotic as everyone packs up their stuff.

"Lee and Shayna, can you both please see me before you head out?" Professor Sherman asks.

After I pack my bag, I reluctantly stand by the podium where the professor is organizing his notes. Lee's large boots clunk as he makes his way down the stairs, smiling and nodding to the people climbing them.

He's wearing a pair of jeans and a snug olive-green Henley that I know for a fact matches the green flecks in his olive eyes. Yes, I'll admit I know that because I've googled him one too many times. His hair is medium brown and longer on top with a natural wave most girls spend hours using a flat iron to achieve. If he wasn't the best football player, he could be a model.

Our eyes briefly meet and he clears his throat when he reaches us. "Hey."

I look back at the professor and he does the same as the professor says, "Lee, as you know, I've been in communication with Coach Buxby. You seem to struggle with some of the material, and since your hours don't work with our tutor clinic the school offers, I've asked Shayna to help you. Lucky for you, she agreed. She has the top grade in this class, and she was in another class of mine, last year. I know she's a hard worker. I have no doubt that if you put in the effort and work with her, your grade will go up."

Lee glances at me and I think he looks a little... embarrassed maybe? I can't be too sure because seconds later, his expression morphs into the same affable one I'm used to seeing on all his social media.

He nods. "Thanks for agreeing to help me."

"Yup," is the only word that comes out of my mouth, which isn't even a proper response to what he said. My cheeks instantly heat.

God, this will be pure torture. I envision myself trying to tutor him, unable to string together a sentence because I'm so nervous.

"I'll leave you two to discuss your schedules and work out a plan of action. If you need my counsel on anything, just let me know." He concentrates more on me than Lee.

I nod and smile, afraid to open my mouth again for fear of something stupid coming out. Then the door slam shuts, the professor leaving us alone in the empty lecture hall.

We stand there trading glances for an awkward beat. My vision goes from my shoes to him and back to my shoes. His confident gaze remains steady on my face the whole time.

"So, what are you thinking? How often do you think we need to get together?" Lee asks.

I struggle to hold his gaze, so I look over his shoulder to make it appear I'm not as uncomfortable as I seem. "I think three times a week to start. If you need more, we can figure it out as we go."

He blows out a breath and cringes, gripping the back of his neck with his hand. "That much, eh?"

The "eh" makes the corner of my lips quirk up. A reminder that he's Canadian.

I shrug. "It's your grade. If you think you can get caught up with two days a week, it's up to you."

His full lips press together. "Nah, I'll make it work. I've gotta pass this class."

"Okay, what days work for you?"

He pulls his phone from his back pocket. I walk over to

the desk beside the podium and set my bag on it to dig out my phone. Lee stands beside me. The scent of his cologne or deodorant or his natural scent reaches me and I close my eyes briefly. I can't identify the scent, but it's crisp and manly and alluring.

"My best options are evenings," he says. "I have practice in the mornings before class. And obviously Saturdays are out because of games, and a lot of Fridays too since we'll be traveling to away games."

I pull up my schedule and frown. A couple of my classes are in the evenings this semester. "How's Sunday work for you? I only have two evenings through the week that can work—Tuesday and Thursday. But there's nowhere else to really squeeze in the third day."

He scrunches up his face in a way that would be cute if he weren't a grown adult male. "Sundays are NFL days." He stares at me as though I should know this.

I understand the NFL plays Sunday, and I'll be giving up watching it as well.

I can't help it. I look at him with an annoyed expression. "Well, it's your grade."

He heaves out a sigh as though the tutoring thing is already interfering with his life too much when I'm the one doing him a favor. Then he nods a few times. "Sundays is it. Can we make it in the afternoon at least? It's my only day to sleep in."

"Sure."

"Where should we meet? I live off campus with my teammate, Miles, so I can't promise that if we study at my place, we won't be in the middle of an NFL marathon party day."

He means Miles Cavanaugh, the team's safety.

"I live in the dorms with a roommate, so we're probably best to meet at the library. I can schedule a private room so we won't disturb anyone else."

"Whoa, Shayna, we just met and you're trying to get me alone?"

My eyes widen and blink a couple of times, my cheeks feeling as if they're on fire.

He chuckles, and the tip of his foot hits the front of my flat. "I'm just kidding. Give me your phone." He holds out his hand.

It takes me a moment to come back before I hand him my phone. He takes it from me, and when his fingers brush over mine, a shock hits us both. I yank my hand away.

"See, we have sparks?" He winks and meets my gaze.

Lord, I can see exactly why so many girls are willing to set aside self-preservation and sleep with this man, knowing he'll probably move on with someone else right after. A girl could get lost in that gaze and wander for eons.

He breaks our staring contest and looks at my phone, his thumbs moving over the screen at a record pace. "Here." He hands back my phone. "I put my contact in there. Just text me when and where to meet you."

"Okay," I choke out.

"Great. Guess I'll see you tomorrow night then. Thanks again." He leaves the room in the same fashion as I imagine he came in—carefree, confident, and without worry.

I wonder what that feels like.

three

. . .

Lee

LATER THAT NIGHT, I'm hanging out with Miles and two other guys from our team, Siska and Bellamoore.

"Dude, you gotta get that grade up. You can't get suspended right before playoffs," Miles says and takes a swig of his smoothie.

We all try to eat pretty clean, but Miles is by far the most obsessive about what goes into his mouth. I swear the guy knows the ingredients and nutritional value of everything that passes his lips.

"Why do you think I have a tutor three times a week now?" I groan and sink back into the couch cushion. "Oh, and my NFL Sundays are gone with it."

This is gonna suck. Any day but Sunday. Not exactly like I can ask her to move her schedule around when she's doing me the favor.

"And Jimmy, the mechanic, is charging me a thousand bucks for the truck repair," I add.

"Shit, man." Miles gives a look of sympathy. We're both only here thanks to a full ride scholarship for football.

"I'll float you," Siska says. He isn't here on full ride. In fact, he was a walk-on our freshman year. There are rumors his daddy bought his spot, but he's a solid player who has saved my back more than once. "Put it on the AMEX."

Miles eyes me because he knows I'll decline, as he would.

"No thanks, man. I just have to man up and ask Kane."

To which Miles frowns. He knows how much I hate the fatherly lectures from my older brother.

"Is your tutor sexy?" Bellamoore changes the subject, thank God.

"Who'd you find to tutor you?" Siska asks, his eyes not leaving the screen as his thumbs pound on the game remote.

"The professor asked some girl in my class. She's got the highest grade in the class."

The three of them laugh and exchange looks.

"What?" I ask.

Miles nods to Bellamoore.

"How long until you're hitting that?" Bellamoore asks but gets distracted when he beats Siska. He stands and declares victory with both arms raised.

I'm willing to let this topic go. I know my track record and why they think the way they do.

"I give him a week tops," Siska says, tossing his remote on the table, sulking from the loss.

I shake my head. "Fuck off. I'm working with her to pass biology, not practice it."

But Shayna does have some damn kissable pouty lips. The way her eyes never focused on me too long made me wonder if she was scared of me or purposely fighting her attraction.

"Sure…" Miles says, and all three of them laugh.

Though I want to be annoyed, I understand where they're coming from. I can't think of any girl I'm strictly friends with. Usually anyone who tries to get to know me wants something from me, whether it's the status of being on my arm or just to brag that they banged the quarterback.

That's not conceit talking; it's reality. But I'm not a dick, so I always make sure they know the score before I bang them. My theory is they do it anyway because they're hoping it's going to be some mind-blowing experience for me and I'll fall in love with them the minute my dick enters their pussy.

So far that risk hasn't paid off for any of them.

"I'm serious. Besides, if you saw her, you'd know she's not like that." I'm lying through my teeth, but they'll never meet her, so it doesn't matter.

"What's she look like?" Siska asks.

I shrug. I didn't give her a second look the first time I saw her in class. But once I was standing across from her, I was struck by her eyes—sort of a mix of blue and green—hiding behind her glasses. And when she spoke, I couldn't help but stare at her lips. And even with her big T-shirt, I was still able to make out the swell of her breasts underneath.

"I don't know. She's nothing special. Kinda geeky, I guess." The words taste sour in my mouth.

"So, she's not impressed by you?" Miles asks.

"Fuck off." I toss an empty pop can sitting on the coffee table at him, but he ducks and it misses him.

"Your turn." Bellamoore holds the controller out to me.

I change the profile on the screen and log myself in, then Siska sets up the next game.

"I'm outta here." Bellamoore stands from the couch and makes his way toward the hallway that leads to the door.

"Where you off to? It's still early," Miles asks.

"Making a stop on the way back to my place." He winks.

"Oh yeah? What's her name?" Siska asks, pressing the button to start the game.

"Kylie. Rylie." He shrugs. "Does it matter? I won't remember in a week."

"You don't remember her name now, dumbass," Siska yells.

The game starts, so we both inch closer to the end of our

seats. Bellamoore flips off Siska behind his back and leaves with the thud of the door closing behind him.

At least the game can distract me from my life problems.

———

That Thursday, I knock lightly on the door of the private library room Shayna texted me to meet her at and hear a soft, "Come in."

I push open the door. She sits at the table, laptop open and papers spread out over the table, pen in hand.

"Hi." Shayna glances quickly at me then back down at her notepad.

"Hey." There are only two chairs in the room: one Shayna sits in and the other one across from her. I step inside, closing the door behind me, then set my bag on the edge of the table before grabbing the other chair and bringing it around the table next to Shayna's.

"Oh," she mumbles.

I pause. "Figured this would be easiest."

She nods, shuffling her papers over to make room for me but never glancing in my direction. "I figured we can start with the first lecture of the semester and work our way through the material from there. I have all my notes here and I printed copies for you. That way we'll see where you're struggling."

"I can answer that—pretty much all of the class." I sit down, unzip my backpack, and pull out my handwritten notes from class, then I plop them down on the table between us.

She takes them and reads through them for a minute, her finger scanning down the margin lines. Which are filled with doodles of small field goals, footballs, robots, and the outline of a woman with breasts and a patch of hair between her legs. What can I say? I get bored and easily distracted in class.

"We have our work cut out for us."

Her words should probably fill me with the fear that I'll never catch up, but I'm too busy studying her face to bother.

Yep, her eyes are definitely aqua colored. The perfect mix of blue and green, like the ocean down in the Caribbean where I spent Christmas with Kane last year. I wish she weren't wearing glasses so I could get a better look at them.

"Let's go through my notes." She hands back my notes and passes hers to me. "You need to let me know if we get to something you don't completely understand and we'll dive in with more depth, okay?"

I find myself nodding, still fixated on her eyes. And when she seems to notice I'm transfixed, her cheeks turn pink and she studies the table.

I clear my throat. "Yeah."

"All right."

For the next two hours, she works her way through her notes, checking in with me to make sure I'm understanding and expanding when I don't quite grasp the idea behind a concept.

She barely meets my eyes, as if I make her nervous. Other than that, she's all business. Not once does she allow the conversation to deviate to anything personal, which bothers me. I'm not even sure why. Isn't that what she's here for? To help me ace this class, not to shoot the shit about unimportant crap?

But a part of me is intrigued by how quiet she is and wants to dig under her protective top layer. What movies does she like? Does she ever go to parties? Is there a wild side of her who likes keg stands and drinking games? Or does she prefer quiet nights in her dorm with a few friends? Most of all, the question I shouldn't care about at all keeps repeating —does she have a boyfriend?

She closes the textbook and slinks back in her chair. "How do you feel about that material?"

"You should be teaching. I understand it a lot better than with Sherman."

A small sound leaks out of her. "I'm glad, so... I'll email you a few questions before we meet Sunday. With your schedule, will you have time to work on them over the next couple of days?"

She says it as if she already knows I have to wake up at five thirty almost every morning to work out, have practice every day with the team, and have to watch tape as well, plus all of my classes and games.

"You a football fan?" If she is, this is my first indication of it. Most girls who follow college ball would have flirted with me all night, knowing exactly who I am. Maybe she likes football, but she's a lesbian?

"Oh. Oh no." She shakes her head vigorously as if I accused her of working at Tassels, the strip club off campus. "No, I just know that college-level athletes must have to dedicate a lot of time, both on and off the field." Shayna shrugs her slender shoulders.

Damn, I might have asked her out if she enjoyed football.

"Right." There's this weird niggling in my belly like maybe she's not telling the truth, but why would she lie? "Yeah, I should be able to handle a couple of questions."

"Great." She pushes back her chair and stands, roughly shoving everything into her backpack as if someone screamed that the first one out gets a million dollars.

I match her pace so that when she's ready to leave, I am too. We exit the room, and rather than walk in silence, I attempt to start a conversation with her.

"You headed home now?" I ask.

"Uh... yeah." She hikes the strap of her bag farther up onto her shoulder.

"Which dorm do you live in?" I match her pace when she seems to walk faster.

"Um..."

She's not exactly a conversationalist. Why am I pushing for more information about her?

"I just meant I'd walk you. You know, it's dark outside and…"

We reach the exit doors.

She shakes her head. "No, I'm not far."

I push a hand through my hair and she tracks the movement, her gaze remaining on my hair for a beat. "I don't really feel right about letting you walk home in the dark."

"I have my rape whistle."

I guess it shouldn't surprise me that this prim and somewhat proper girl is always prepared. She must have been a Girl Scout. When my pen ran out while we were working, she offered me one of her extras—all categorized by ink color and point diameter.

She unzips the front pocket of her backpack, pulls out a whistle, and slips the cord over her head, so it hangs right in front of her breasts. I try not to notice the way her sweater indents, but it's hard. Impossible really.

"All right, well… keep your phone handy in case you run into trouble."

She kind of looks at me as though I'm a creep, so I back off. It still doesn't feel right to just let her walk on her own. But maybe she has a jealous boyfriend or something.

"Yep, well… okay. I'll see you Sunday." Without waiting for me to answer, she spins on her heel and walks down the steps of the building, taking the path to the left.

For some reason, I stand there watching until she's out of sight.

The sound of my name being shouted pulls me from my trance.

"Burrows! Hey, Lee!"

Miles and Siska are standing on the grass near the path, lit by one of the pathway lights.

I jog down the stairs and over to them. "Hey, what's up?"

"That your tutor?" Miles asks, glancing in the direction that Shayna went.

"Yeah, that's her."

"Fuck, man. What, are you blind? She's not half bad." Siska lightly smacks me in the stomach. "What? Were you afraid we were going to try to tap it before you?"

I shake my head. "She's not like that."

"You're fucking with us. She's got that hot librarian look going on." Siska licks his lips as if he's imagining thrusting inside her.

The mere idea of that makes my hands clench into fists. I shake my head and walk in the direction of my apartment.

Siska catches up to me with a quick jog. "I mean it, man. Why else wouldn't you go after that? She has that sweet and innocent look I know you love. You telling me you don't want to dirty her up?" He throws his arm around my shoulders and I slide away.

I grind my molars together. The way he's talking about her pisses me off, but I can't exactly say or show that to him. It's never bothered me before when he talks like that about girls. How would I explain why it does now when I don't understand it myself?

"Maybe I should show you how it's done?" Siska clamps a hand on my shoulder, and I jerk away.

The idea of him seducing Shayna makes me want to pound him into the ground.

"Don't bother," I mutter.

I glance at Miles. He's biting the inside of his cheek like he does when he's uncomfortable.

"You like her," Siska says.

"No." I shake my head and jog across the street.

"Just go home, Siska." Miles attempts to stop where this is going.

"If you don't like her, then let me to slip into her DMs. Give me her info."

Siska's fucking insane if he thinks that's going to happen.

"I'm not giving you her information."

His manic laugh echoes through the night air. He's the type of guy who always gets what he wants, and he never accepts defeat. Which means he's never going to let this topic go. I wish I would have kept the tutor thing all to myself.

Then there's silence and I walk faster to get to my apartment.

"Then let's make a bet." Siska places a hand on my shoulder and I stop walking. "I bet I can sleep with her before you."

"Fuck, Siska." Miles runs a hand down his face.

I love Siska like a brother, but the guy sleeps with more girls than any of us. He shows them zero respect. I don't want Shayna exposed to that.

"Hell no. Don't go near her." My voice comes out more forceful, giving up my feelings for her. Not feelings per se, but the fact I don't want him touching her.

Siska nods a few times, his eyes on me. "Okay then… I'll bet you can't sleep with her before the end of your tutoring sessions."

I scoff and shake my head. "I'm not betting you about this. Shit, man, this is my fucking football career in jeopardy."

Siska grins. "Guess you'd better take me up on that bet then. Unless you want me to corrupt your pretty, sweet tutor."

It feels as if a shark is gnawing at my insides.

I widen my stance and cross my arms. "And what do I get once I prove to you I can get any girl to sleep with me, including my tutor?"

That arrogant grin needs to be stripped from his face. "I'll pay to get your truck out of Jimmy's Auto."

"Free and clear?" Miles asks for me. "No paybacks?"

"Of course. But if you don't get her into bed before the end of the tutoring sessions, she's all mine afterward."

I lock eyes with Miles, and he raises his eyebrows. I have no idea if Shayna is interested in me. There were a few signs that would make me think she is, but I'm definitely going into this bet blind, which isn't me. I'm not even a betting kind of guy.

I stick out my hand. "Fine. Deal."

Siska hoots, but I don't feel any elation. In fact, I feel like a dick. Regardless of the fact that I'm trying to save Shayna from Siska seducing her and tossing her aside, nothing about this feels as if I'm doing her a favor.

four

. . .

Shayna

I'M LYING on my bed in my dorm room, staring at a picture of Lee on my wall. It's the one they sold at the end of last year when the team made the National Championship.

He's different than I thought he'd be. So far, he's been attentive and asked questions. I assumed I'd be trying to get him to be active in the discussion and he'd offer me something to sit next to him so he could cheat. I know how the prominent athletes sometimes don't earn their grades.

I mean, sure, Lee's affable and easygoing and sometimes he tried to steer the conversation to anything not biology related, but that was after an hour or more. There's no question his goal is passing this class and not getting suspended from the team. Which is how he's gotten so far with his football career to date.

But he's not the pompous, egotistical jerk I thought he'd be, given the fact he's treated like a god on this campus. Which makes me feel a little less like an idiot for the giant crush I've had on him since orientation.

I might be what some consider a geek, but I'm a closet

football fan for most who know me. In fact, I never miss a game. I'm that fan in the stands decked out in blue and yellow face paint and waving yellow pom-poms. Occasionally, I even wear a yellow wig.

I'm not sure why I lied when Lee asked if I was a football fan. I just felt like I'd be giving him too much access to my true self if I admitted that I never miss a home game. Even on the weeks I have to go on my own because I can't convince my friends to join me.

The alarm on my phone goes off and I silence it. Time to head to the library to meet Lee. It's Sunday, so we have the whole day to study together. I try to push away the thrill that races through my belly at the idea of spending the day with him. It's stupid. I mean, I can barely look him in the eye.

Once I've packed all my stuff, I head to the library and straight to the same room. When I open the door, I expect to be alone, but I startle and yelp when I see Lee is already sitting behind the desk.

He chuckles. "Sorry. Didn't mean to scare you."

My hand presses to my chest where my heart beats rapidly. "I just didn't expect you to be here first."

"I'm full of surprises." He grins. There's a hint of flirtation in his smile and the way he said the words, but I could be hearing things. Why would Lee Burrows flirt with me?

Instead of having a smart comeback like an interesting person, my boring self comes into the light. "Give me a minute to get settled, then we can start."

I walk over to the desk and set down my backpack, pulling out papers and arranging them on the table while Lee watches me.

"Aren't you going to congratulate me?"

I look at him and see his winning smile. It makes his hazel and green eyes sparkle in a way that seems mischievous.

"On what?" I feign ignorance, knowing he's probably talking about the game yesterday.

"My stellar game yesterday. Four touchdowns." He holds up his hand with four fingers in the air. Oh man, he's gorgeous.

I look away and pull out my laptop and sign in. "Is that good?"

He scoffs. "'Is that good?' she asks. Hell yeah, it's good."

I shrug. "Congratulations then, I guess. Are you ready to get started?"

Lee tilts his head and studies me for a beat before he nods, reaching for his pen. Of course he can't keep his enthusiasm at bay—it was an incredible game. He probably went out last night and celebrated with some hot blonde with big breasts who woke up in his bed this morning.

We spend the next hour going through my lecture notes. He gets stuck on a few concepts, but I'm able to talk him through them. I know he's here on a full ride scholarship, but he's certainly not all brawn and no brains. He's holding his own pretty well.

When I break to grab my drink from my bag, he uses the opportunity to shift the conversation. I loosen the cap on my lemonade and take a sip.

"Do you have a boyfriend?" he asks.

My throat involuntarily clenches and I cough and sputter, dangerously close to spitting lemonade all over either him or the table. Lee rubs my back. Holy shit.

To my dismay, my nipples pebble in my bra, but I hope he doesn't notice because of the baggy sweatshirt I'm wearing.

"You all right?" Genuine concern is etched on his face.

I nod and replace the cap on my drink. "Fine. Yeah. Wrong pipe."

He drops his hand, and as much as I shouldn't, because there's no way anything will ever happen between us, I'd use a million genie wishes for him to put it back.

"So? Do you?" He looks at me intently.

"Why do you want to know?" I must scowl at him because he chuckles.

"Just curious. We're stuck together for a while, and I guess I figured we'd get to know one another."

"Do you have a girlfriend?" I'm pretty sure the answer is no. Even with my lame social standing, the rumors of all the girls he's been with over the past two plus years still reach me.

He shakes his head. "No. Too busy with football to be a decent boyfriend to anyone."

I nod even though I'll bet that's not the only reason. I'm sure Lee enjoys all the attention he garners and the ease with which his status as a football god gets him into girls' pants.

"I don't have a boyfriend," I mutter, not sure if he still cares at this point.

"Huh."

"What's that supposed to mean?" I glance at him.

"Just surprised, that's all. Figured a girl like you would."

I turn in my chair and my eyes narrow. "A girl like me?" I arch an eyebrow.

He laughs again and puts up his hands. "You know… pretty, stable, smart, obviously going places in life." He raises a shoulder.

Did Lee Burrows call me pretty? Oh my God, he did. Please hold me before I faint.

My cheeks heat and I know he notices because he says, "You sure are shy, aren't you?"

I glance away from him. "I'm not shy."

He chuckles. "You can't even look me in the eye half the time."

"I can too." Though it's not lost on me that I'm not looking at him now and my voice sounded like a four-year-old version of myself telling my older brother that I could go down the big kid slide too.

He stands and situates his chair so it's facing me. When I

don't turn my chair, he puts his hands at the edge of my chair and turns it with me on it.

"Okay, let's see how long you can lock eyes with me. Look at me." He uses two fingers to point toward his eyes.

"This is ridiculous," I mutter but participate, nonetheless.

Our eyes lock and hold. The urge to glance away is immediate, but I force myself to keep looking at him. The tension between us pulls tighter and tighter until it's like an elastic band at its max stretchability.

My breathing grows shallow and my heart pounds like a metronome that keeps getting faster and faster. Eventually I can't take it anymore and I break eye contact.

"Ha! Told you." He points at me.

Embarrassment spreads through me, and I bet if I looked in a mirror right now, even my neck would be red. "Whatever. So what? That doesn't mean I'm shy. Maybe you're just too ugly to look at for that long?"

He smiles that winning grin that gets him all the girls. "We both know that isn't true."

"Arrogance," I say, picking up some papers.

He nudges me with his elbow. "I didn't say it was a bad thing. I kinda like you not ogling me all the time."

"Ogle?"

His shoulders lift, then he pulls up his shirt. "The abs. They love the abs."

The shirt drops way too fast before I can commit his body to memory. Damn him.

I don't want to get ideas—crazy ideas like maybe he could actually like me, because this definitely feels a little flirtatious. Then again, I'd bet my entire grade in biology that the man doesn't even know he's flirting.

I grab the textbook and flip to the next page. "Why don't we get back to work? We have that test coming up and a lot of ground to cover still."

He sighs and shifts his chair closer to the table. "All right, boss. What are we working on next?"

We spend the next couple hours working until I can tell that Lee's brain is at capacity overload. He's no longer focused and is finding it harder to retain information, so I suggest that we pack up for the day.

He agrees, and we leave the library together. As I notice the people in the library watch us, I can't imagine the life he leads. Even if he wasn't the star quarterback, they'd probably stare at Lee for his model looks alone.

Today he's wearing a pair of athletic pants and a hoodie with his coat, and he pulls a beanie onto his head once we're walking out the exit.

"Thanks for your help today. It's starting to all make sense," he says when we reach the top of the stairs outside. It's cold enough that I see faint white traces of his breath in the air.

"If you have any problems with the questions I gave you, just text me before our session on Tuesday."

"Will do."

"Burrows!" sounds from the bottom of the stairs.

We both turn in the direction of his name, and I recognize Miles Cavanaugh, Damon Siska, and Travis Bellamoore. All Lee's teammates.

He blows out a long breath. "C'mon." He nods. "I'll introduce you to the guys."

For whatever reason, he doesn't seem exactly happy about it, even though he offered. Is he embarrassed to be seen with me?

"That's okay. I should get going. I still have some schoolwork to catch up on." Lie. I finished most of my work on Friday night. What I didn't get to, I finished on Saturday morning before the afternoon football game.

Lee gives me a small scowl and it's the first time I've ever seen him look annoyed. "You can spare two minutes to say hello. C'mon."

I follow him down the steps and notice the way the guys watch me with avid interest. Nervous, I push my glasses farther up on my face.

When we reach the bottom of the stairs, Lee gestures toward me. "Guys, this is Shayna Kudrow. Shayna, this is Miles, Damon, and Travis. They all play on the team with me."

I smile and nod, not sure what to do. I try to act as if I don't know who these guys are because I told Lee I don't follow football, but in reality, I know all these guys' stats, let alone their names. "Hi."

"So, you're the one trying to help our boy here pass biology?" Miles gives Lee a shove, who shoves him back. There's nothing aggressive about it though. It appears brotherly.

"That's me." I turn to Lee. "I better go. I have lots of work to do still."

"Okay, I'll see you Tuesday."

I press my lips together and nod, then turn on my heel and head toward my dorm, trying to leave behind all thoughts of Lee.

five

· · ·

Lee

A COUPLE OF WEEKS PASS, and Shayna continues to tutor me. As my knowledge in biology grows with each study session, so does my interest in her.

She intrigues me with how guarded and quiet she is. Totally unlike the girls I'm used to, who have no problem hitting on me or telling me exactly what they want from me—usually me between their legs.

And Shayna's so smart. It turns me on. I could listen to her explain cardiac electrophysiology all day long.

Something tells me that under her glasses, ponytail, and baggy shirts lies a woman who is hot as hell but is afraid to let herself run wild. I kinda like the idea of being the one who sees her like that.

But the bet I made with Siska has me second-guessing the idea of pursuing her. I'm not a cruel person and playing with her feelings when I know I don't want anything serious with anyone feels cruel. Sure, I said yes to the bet, but I never really planned on following through. Honestly, I thought they'd forget all about it, but ever since they met Shayna that day outside the library, they ask me every Tuesday, Thursday, and Sunday whether I've sealed the deal with her yet.

I'm getting sick of listening to them talk about how I'm losing my touch. Especially since I haven't gotten laid in weeks. It's not that there haven't been offers, but every time I try to make myself pursue something with a willing girl, Shayna's face flashes through my mind and I can't do it. It wouldn't be fair to the other girl if I was fucking her and pretending she was Shayna.

Still, the guys have effectively cockblocked me with this stupid bet—unless I want to tell Shayna about it.

Maybe I could? Maybe I could explain to her how I'm feeling but how I'm conflicted because of the bet? She'd probably think I'm a douchebag for agreeing to the bet in the first place, then she wouldn't be into me anymore.

Because I think she might be into me.

I remember the way her cheeks pinkened that day I asked if she had a boyfriend and called her pretty and smart. And I've noticed the way she won't meet my eyes but will steal looks at me when she thinks I'm not looking.

Whatever. If I want my truck fixed, I have to pursue her or bury my tail between my legs and ask Kane, who will lecture me for the next four months about money and how I should have been working my ass off this summer. Regardless, Shayna isn't the kind of girl who's looking to sleep together and nothing more. And I meant it when I said I was too busy with football and school to have a steady girlfriend.

I decide to stop in at the café before I head to the library. I have a little extra time. Lately I've been showing up before our study session is due to start, like some eager beaver.

I'm about to order when I spot Shayna outside the doors of the café, talking to a guy. I don't recognize him—not that I would. Our school is pretty big. Still, I can't help but stiffen when she laughs at something he says.

I never noticed her before she started tutoring me, but

now it feels as though everywhere I look, there she is. As if I'm programmed to hone in on her location if she's nearby. The other day, I spotted her walking across campus. I knew it was her just from the gait of her walk before she was even close enough for me to see her face.

By the time I exit the café, she's gone. I frown and make my way to the library, finding her inside our usual room, waiting.

"I saw you at the café. Who was that guy you were talking to?" The question drops like vomit after twenty tequila shots. What the hell? I sound like a jealous stalker.

She stills from setting up her things on the table. "What? Raymond? He's a classmate of mine. Why?"

Feeling like an idiot, I shrug and close the door. "Just wondering." I unpack everything I need from my backpack and settle in. "Ready to do this?"

She bites her bottom lip and nods, pulling her textbook forward. About a half hour later, she's showing me something on her laptop when a notification pops up that she has a new email message. I hear her quick intake of breath.

"What?" I look at her, confused.

"Our biology test results are in."

My stomach flips. We had our test last week. Though I know I did a hell of a lot better than I would have if she weren't tutoring me, I'm not sure I did well enough to earn a decent grade.

She eyes my bag. "Get your computer and see what your grade is."

I slide my backpack across the table, my arms feeling like lead as dread spreads through me. What if I didn't pass? What if I can't do well in this class even with Shayna helping me? Which means, I don't play this Saturday.

I open my laptop and pull up the university's portal, logging in. My finger hovers over the return key once my cursor is blinking on the biology class button.

"What are you waiting for?" She's positioned at the edge of her seat as though she can't wait to see my results. As though she's somehow confident that she's an expert tutor and I did well. I wish I had the same confidence. Not as her skills of a tutor—she's killer—but my brain had to process all that information correctly for me to do well.

"What if I flunked? I'll be riding the bench the rest of the season." My jaw tightens.

"There's no way you failed, Lee. You were in a good position heading into the test."

It's the surety in her voice that spurs me to press the return key. It's probably only seconds, but it feels like minutes while the screen changes. And when it reveals the course page listing my marks, I see eighty-two percent marked on the last test.

Holy shit, I did it.

"Woohoo!" I stand with my fists in the air and turn to face Shayna. I pull her up, wrapping my arms around her. "We did it!"

"I knew you could," she says against my shoulder and squeezes me tightly.

We're both so elated that it takes a minute for us to come to our senses and realize we're pressed against each other with our arms wrapped around one another. I can tell the instant she registers our position because she stiffens in my arms, and a whine runs up my throat, willing her to go soft and pliant again. She pulls back, but instead of dropping my arms completely, I don't.

She glances up and our eyes meet. Shayna's breathing so hard her breasts push against my chest with each inhale.

We breathe each other in. She feels so good in my arms, and no moment has felt more right than this one. As though I'm being pulled in like a fish on a hook, I lean down until I'm millimeters from her lips and close my eyes.

A knock on the door startles us both and we spring apart.

The librarian opens the door and assesses us with a stern glare. "Everything okay in here? Thought I heard some yelling."

"Everything is fine," Shayna says in a shaky voice. She's so transparent. Her face is red with embarrassment.

The librarian gives us a thorough look, nods, and closes the door.

I open my mouth to address what almost happened with Shayna, but she beats me to it. "We should finish up. We only have the room for another hour."

I clear my throat and adjust my stance because I'm bearing a half-chub. Shayna pretends not to notice. "Yeah… sure."

She nods, a short assertive movement, and I return the gesture and sit.

Probably for the best anyway. Hurting this girl is not on the list of achievements I'm aiming for when it comes to records in college. There's a reason I'm transparent with every girl. I never want a woman to bear heartbreak at my hands.

———

Saturday comes—game day. We're playing Ohio State, our biggest rivals, so tensions are high and the pressure bears down on me like a car crusher.

Coach gave us his best pep talk and I've watched so much game tape this week my eyes are crossed, but I feel ready, like we're going to win.

We score the only touchdown in the first half of the game, and after half time, we come out more determined to win. About halfway through the third quarter, Ohio's coach calls a time-out, so we rush to the sideline.

Coach Buxby is going over the next play we're going to run, and as I listen, I glance up at the screen. The cameras are panning from one fan to another, showing off some of their crazy outfits and face paint since this is the game of the year for us. Even when we play Ohio at their home field, most of our school makes the trip.

It's a sea of blue and yellow, shirtless guys with painted chests and heads, but the camera pauses on a familiar face.

At first, I second-guess myself. No way it's her. It's not Shayna.

Her face is painted blue with twin yellow Ms on her cheeks and she has a crazy yellow wig on, but I'd recognize those glasses anywhere. Not to mention the smile as she waves around yellow pom-poms.

But her smile drops the moment she realizes her image is being broadcast to the whole stadium. In true Shayna fashion, she sits in apparent embarrassment and shields her face. The camera moves on to the next person, but I can't help the slow grin that spreads across my face.

Not a football fan, my ass.

"Burrows, you listening?" Coach yells.

I blink and give my head a shake for a second. "Give it to me again, Coach?"

"Jesus. How the hell do you expect to win? No wonder you threw that interception in the second."

My teeth grind together. His words and Shayna's presence are enough to narrow my focus back on the game. I'm supposed to be a leader and I hate the rare occasion when Coach has to call me out on something. And now that I know Shayna's watching, I'm more determined than ever to win this game.

And win we do. It's by a narrower margin than I would have liked, but a win is a win.

Now I can't wait to see Shayna tomorrow.

six

. . .

Shayna

I TEXTED Lee first thing this morning to let him know that the library had a flood overnight and we won't be able to use the usual room for our study session today. He suggested that we meet at his place off campus. Apparently, his roommate, Miles, stayed at some girl's place last night and Lee isn't expecting him home until late afternoon.

I reluctantly agreed. Not because I don't trust Lee. Not at all. I just think it'll feel weird not being in public with him. Especially after what I'm pretty sure was an almost kiss the other day.

I'm still riding high from our win over Ohio, so I can't imagine how he's feeling. I wonder if he was up all night partying. I was mortified when I saw myself on the screen, but he was busy in the huddle, so there's no way he saw me. I just hope he doesn't record the games and watch them.

It doesn't take me too long to walk over to his place, and thankfully, it's a mild day. This is my favorite time of year on campus. I love when the leaves change color and the air is crisp. Halloween is next weekend, and so far, the days have been pretty sunny and mild this month. It's only at night that the temperature drops enough that you can see your breath.

I locate the small apartment building, walk up the stairs to the third floor of the triplex, and knock on the door. It only takes Lee a minute to answer the door. His hair is wet and he's shirtless with athletic pants on. My gaze snags on the muscles in his chest and the trail of hair leading down past his waistband.

Wow.

I mean, I knew he was fit, obviously. But seeing it live and in person is something else.

"Hey, sorry," he says casually, as though nothing is amiss. "I just got out of the shower when you knocked. Let me go grab a shirt. Why don't you head into the living room?" He gestures down the hall behind him to the right.

"Okay. Sure."

When he turns, I squeeze my eyes shut, trying to get the image of him shirtless out of my head, but I'm fairly sure it's been tattooed to the insides of my eyelids.

When he returns, I have my computer and notes out and I'm ready to go. Today I plan to do a review of everything we've covered so far and take a look at what he's already worked on for the assignment that's due next week.

We get to work right away, but about a half hour in, he interrupts to ask if I want anything to drink. "Sorry, I should've offered when you first got here."

"Some water would be great."

"Sure." He pushes up off the couch.

I watch him walk barefoot across the room into the open kitchen. Since when do I think that bare feet are sexy? Since I saw Lee Burrows.

I really need to date more. I think all work and no play has taken a toll on me.

"Here you go." He hands me a cold bottle of water and

cracks open his own, slugs some back, then sits beside me again. "Actually, I'll be right back. I forgot something."

He jets down the hall again and returns with something behind his back and a mischievous grin on his face. "So…"

When he doesn't continue, I look up at him. "So?"

"All Michigan football fans should have a flag to wave." He pulls a Michigan flag from behind his back and waves it.

Shit.

I stiffen. "I'm not a fan," I respond casually, trying to keep my voice even.

"Huh." He sits on the couch. "Could have sworn I saw you yesterday."

I groan and let my chin drop to my chest as Lee laughs. He's got a great laugh. Deep, contagious, and genuine.

"Aw, don't be embarrassed, shy pie. I thought you looked cute with the yellow wig."

I bury my head in my hands. "Shy pie?"

"Yeah." He shrugs. "I think it suits you."

Oh my God. Lee Burrows just gave me a nickname. Freshman me would die, but twenty-year-old me manages to keep it together.

"So why wouldn't you just tell me you're a college football fan?" he asks, laying the flag down by my bag.

I slump back into the couch, tossing my pen on the coffee table. "I don't know. I didn't want to feed your ego, I guess? Probably everyone you come into contact with practically worships you. I didn't want you to think you'd get away with things from me." I shrug because I don't really have a clear answer.

"Shayna." The way he says my name has me twisting my neck to look at him. His gaze is hot and solid on mine. "You're not like any girl I've ever known."

My breath stutters to a stop in my throat. Lee cups my cheek, and I can't help but melt into the moment, my eyes drifting closed.

"Shayna, I really want to kiss you right now. Would that be all right?"

I know I should say no. I definitely should. But I can't let an opportunity like this pass me by, so I give him a small nod. But it's enough for Lee to understand, because when I open my eyes, he's bringing his lips to mine.

He cups the side of my face again and brushes his lips over mine tentatively. I arch my back so I can get closer, and he does it again. The third time he kisses me, his tongue coasts over the seam of my lips. A soft moan leaves my mouth and I open for him.

His tongue explores my mouth. Slowly at first, then with increased vigor. Our tongues tangle and soon I'm lying on the couch with the weight of his body over mine. His arousal presses into me between my thighs and my legs spread so that he's wedged between them. We jut our hips back and forth, dry humping in our search for friction.

Every part of me feels extra sensitive where we touch, and when he brings one of his hands down on my chest and grips my breast in his large palm, I almost cry out. His touch feels so good. Shocks of sensation travel from my breast to my core, where I clench.

Lee's hand slides up under the hem of my sweatshirt and tugs down the cup of my bra. His finger and thumb immediately find my nipple, and he tweaks the puckered bud, causing pleasure to ripple throughout my body.

I can't get enough. Somewhere in the back of my mind, I know I should stop, but all I can think is more, more, more. Never in a million years did I think we'd end up like this.

We kiss until the sexual tension filling the room is suffocating. When he pulls back and looks down at me, his lids are heavy and his lips are swollen. He looks every bit the sexual man I'm sure he is and being the one who created that look feels powerful.

"I want you so bad, shy pie." He punctuates his words

with a press of his hips that pushes the end of his hard length into the perfect spot.

Silly man. The use of the nickname he's given me is aphrodisiac enough. But I force myself to really think about this before I rip off his clothes.

My hands run down his shoulders to his biceps. "Lee, I'm just not someone who can sleep with someone and not have it mean anything." My voice is strangled and I don't sound confident in my decision. Because I *am* unsure.

Truth is, I want to sleep with him, but I don't want to be just another notch on his headboard. Even if he is Lee Burrows, University of Michigan starting quarterback.

His hands continue to run across my body. "I wasn't lying when I said I don't have time to be a decent boyfriend to someone."

I nod, understanding and appreciating his honesty, though I'd be lying if I said I'm not disappointed we're not on the same page. When I start to slide out from under him, he gently presses my shoulder back to the couch cushion.

"But I'll try for you. I won't be around twenty-four seven, but I like you, Shayna. I meant it when I said I think you're pretty and smart, and I like spending time with you. I want to do more of it, but I don't have that much time to give. But I'll give you what I can if that's okay with you."

I want to look under me or over me or to the side of me. Surely, he's talking to someone else in the room. Lee Burrows wants to try to have a relationship with me? Elation courses through my veins, and I wrap my arms around his neck and pull him toward me, kissing him.

Things get heated again in no time, and within minutes, he's carrying me to his bedroom, my legs wrapped around his waist. He closes the door with his foot and reaches behind him while we keep kissing to lock the door. Then he deposits me on the bed.

The nerves hit when he stands, his erection tenting his

pants, and rakes his gaze down my body. I'm not a virgin, but I've only been with two other guys and those times were "meh" at best. Lee is experienced and I'm sure he knows what he's doing, much more than I do.

"Relax. I can see you getting all up in your head. We're not going to do anything you don't want to, okay?"

I nod. That's the thing. I want to.

I mean, I *really* want to.

I just want him to enjoy it also.

"Can I take off your shirt and bra?" he asks.

"Only if you take off yours," I say, remembering his bare chest from earlier.

Without breaking eye contact, he reaches behind his neck and pulls off his shirt with one fluid motion. The shirt floats to the floor.

Oh, yeah. We are so doing this. The man is built like a god.

Lee gives me a chaste kiss, then gently lifts my sweatshirt up over my head. My bra is next to go, and I sit on the edge of the bed, biting my bottom lip and hoping he likes what he sees.

"I can't wait to feel you come around my cock." He grins and drops to his knees in front of me.

Based on the look on his face when he licks his lips, I know—it's on.

seven

. . .

Lee

GOD, she is so fucking perfect.

I knew as soon as my lips touched hers that I was fucked.

Why she hides this body of hers under baggy shirts and sweaters, I'll never know. But I'd be lying if I said I wasn't pleased to be one of what I think is probably only a handful of guys to unwrap her.

A moment of hesitation hits me where I wonder if I should stop what I'm doing and tell her about the bet. But the damn bet has no place here. It's not why I'm doing this. Not at all. We can talk about it later. Or never.

I lean in and draw her nipple into my mouth. Her hand goes into my hair, and she moans. The sound makes my cock push against the inside of my pants even more than it already is. I want to hear her make that sound when I'm deep inside her.

Once I have her thoroughly worked up and practically keening, I stand. "Shimmy up the bed."

She does what I ask without question. It feels sort of like a gift, the way she trusts me. I don't get the feeling she trusts many people easily.

I walk over to my nightstand and open the top drawer, pull out a condom, and toss it on the bed, then I get to work removing my pants and boxer briefs. Normally I'd be into a bit of foreplay, but I cannot wait any longer. I've wanted between this girl's legs for weeks now. Besides, if we're dating, there will be lots of opportunities to explore each other's bodies thoroughly down the road.

When I drop my pants and underwear, my dick springs free, and Shayna's aqua eyes widen.

"You like what I'm working with?" I can't help but be cocky. It's not the first time a woman has been impressed by my package.

"Seems like you're working with a lot."

"Don't worry, shy pie. You're gonna love it." I get on the mattress and crawl over to her, zeroing in on my target and pulling down her jogging pants.

Since she started tutoring me, I've wondered about a thousand times what type of underwear this practical girl might wear, but never would I have thought I'd find a red lace thong under her clothes.

"Did you wear these hoping I'd see them?"

"I like nice undies. Sue me." Her confidence only makes me harder.

"Well, I love these… but I'm afraid they gotta go." I slip my fingers under the thin strap on each side of her hips and slowly pull them down to reveal a small patch of dark-blonde hair between her legs.

God, I wanna run my tongue between her legs, but my cock is painfully throbbing. I need to be inside her.

Reaching for the condom, I ask her, "You sure about this?"

She nods. "Yeah, I want you."

I rip the package off with my teeth and roll the condom on before situating myself between her legs. Our eyes meet as I inch inside her. Fuck, she's tight. So tight. I might bust a nut before I get all the way in.

I work myself in slowly, and once I'm fully seated inside her, I still to give her a moment to get used to my size and so I can compose myself and not make this an unsatisfying experience for her.

"You good?" I ask when I can barely bear any longer without movement.

"Yeah." She nods.

Leaning in, I kiss her and feel against my cock how it makes her insides twitch.

Fuck, that's so hot.

I move slowly at first, and when I can tell how wet she is, I go faster. The sound of slapping skin fills the room, as well as her soft pants. My cock is like granite, and each thrust in and out of her is like a little piece of heaven.

Shayna's nails dig into my ass as she urges me on, and I groan. Her tits bounce with every thrust and I watch her eyes grow heavy with lust. Without warning, I roll us over so she's on top.

"Oh." She stares down at me, hands pressed to my chest.

"I wanna watch you fuck me. Take what you want, Shayna." I reach up and around her head and pull out her ponytail holder, tossing it to the floor.

Jesus. The boys were right. Hot librarian is the perfect description for her right now, looking down at me with swollen lips, disheveled hair, and her glasses still on.

She moves tentatively at first, but I urge her on with a light smack to her ass. My shy pie doesn't want to show me what she needs, but I want her to take everything she desires.

Her movements become more intentional and stronger until she's riding my cock like a porn star, her ample tits swaying and bouncing. When I can tell she's close, I pinch her right nipple and use the thumb of my other hand to zero in on her clit. She throws her head back and moans, grinding down onto my thumb, and when she comes with a cry and she tries to milk my cock, I can't hold back any longer.

I push up into her rapid fire and come with a roar.

Damn. I knew we'd be good together, but I didn't know we'd be *that* good.

She slumps forward and I run my hands up and down the bare skin of her back while she catches her breath. Eventually she rolls off of me. I stand, pulling off the condom and tying it before depositing it in the garbage can by my desk.

From the bed, Shayna watches me warily while I make my way back over to her.

"What's up?" I frown.

She shyly tilts her legs so I can no longer see her pussy, and she covers her tits with her forearm. "I don't usually do this. I'm not sure what to do."

I chuckle and crawl back onto the bed. "You don't have to do anything. Let's just lie here and enjoy the post-orgasmic glow." I draw her into me so that her cheek lays on my chest and my hand rests on her hip.

We're quiet for a few minutes, probably both thinking about what we did and wondering when we can do it again. Or maybe that's just me.

"Hey, we're having a Halloween party here next Saturday night after we get back from the game. You wanna come?"

She shifts and looks up at me. "Really?"

"Yeah, really. I meant what I said. I don't have a lot of time, but I'll give you what I can. You have to dress up though."

She looks uncertain but then nods decisively. "Yeah, I'll come."

"Great." I tilt her chin up and kiss her lips.

The sound of the apartment door slamming makes us both still.

"Who is that?" she whispers.

My forehead creases. "Must be Miles. I didn't think he'd be home this early."

Shayna sits up and covers her breasts. "Oh my God. I have to get out of here."

I wish I could say it doesn't bother me that she's so concerned someone might know we slept together, but I know she's not used to this kind of thing. She probably doesn't want my best friend's first impression of her to be that she warms my bed whenever I snap my fingers.

"Give him a minute. He'll probably go to the kitchen, then head to his bedroom to nap for a couple hours before games start. That's his usual routine."

Sure enough, I hear some cupboards in the kitchen open and close a few times, followed by the sound of his bedroom door shutting. The second it does, Shayna bolts out of bed and gathers her things, putting them back on as fast as humanly possible.

"You don't need to rush out of here." I sit up and reach for my athletic pants on the floor and pull them on.

"Yes, I do. I don't want your friend to see me like this." She redoes her hair into a ponytail and pushes her glasses up.

I follow her out of my room and back to the living room, where she hurriedly shoves her things in her backpack. I wrap my arms around her waist and pull her toward me.

"I'll see you Tuesday night?" I arch an eyebrow because the way she's rushing out of here is giving me serious "I think I made a mistake" vibes.

She wiggles out of my hold and swings her backpack up onto her shoulder. "Yeah, Tuesday. See you then."

And then she's off, rushing down the hall and leaving my apartment before I can say another word.

I decide not to worry too much about it. She just didn't want to make a bad impression. Things will be fine once we're out together at the party on Saturday. Then everyone will know where we stand—together.

eight

. . .

Shayna

I *SLEPT* WITH LEE BURROWS.

I'm *dating* Lee Burrows.

Lee Burrows *likes* me.

I have to keep repeating the words because they're too unbelievable. Even after we slept together last Sunday.

I felt like a bit of an idiot rushing out of his place like that, but I didn't want his roommate to see me and think I'm like all the other girls who want to brag that I banged the quarterback.

Yes, I want to shout it off the rooftops, but I haven't told anyone. I believed Lee when he said he wants to try to see if we can have a relationship, but I want to make sure things are solid before I go telling everyone.

Lee insists that the party tonight is our coming out. We'll see. The past week he coerced me into sitting up in his row during class. Sadly, it didn't take much convincing. I have at least been able to draw the line clear during tutoring. The team lost today, so I'm sure they're all in crappy moods. Maybe he won't feel like it anymore.

After one last check in the mirror to make sure my Ruth Bader Ginsberg costume is on point, I grab my jacket and head out. By the time I reach his apartment, my stomach feels as if it's doing pirouettes. The last time I was this nervous was on the first day of our tutoring sessions. And look how that turned out, right? I should relax. Tonight, will be fun.

The music and loud voices can be heard walking up the stairs, and I knock harder than I normally would. After about a minute, Miles answers the door dressed like Richard Simmons. I chuckle. I guess Lee wasn't kidding when he said that Miles is really into fitness and nutrition.

"Hey! Shayla, right?" He smiles, beer in hand.

"Shayna, actually."

"Right. Shayna. Sorry. Come in." He opens the door wider and motions for me to join the party, so I walk past him. "I think Burrows is in the kitchen."

"Great, thanks."

"Can I get you a beer or something?" he asks loud enough to be heard over the music.

"I think I'll just find Lee first." I smile, trying not to seem as though I don't deserve to be here. This has never been my crowd.

"Kitchen, like I said." He points and heads off down the hallway toward the living room/kitchen combo.

I follow and stand in the doorway. The place is packed with people filling every corner, and I see some mingling farther down the hall near the bedrooms too. It takes me a minute to spot him, but I do catch a glimpse of Lee in the kitchen, so I make my way over.

No one pays me any attention as I weave through the masses. A lot of the guys I recognize as players on the team, and I don't know any of the girls. I don't have many friends, and most of the ones I do would never be at this party.

I reach the kitchen and see Lee in his Where's Waldo

costume—red beanie with red-and-white-striped shirt, jeans, and glasses that look a lot like my own.

As though he can feel my presence, Lee glances away from the guy he's talking to and finds me. The smile that splits his handsome face makes me lightheaded.

He says something to the guy then pushes his way over to me. "Hey, you look great."

"Thanks. So do you." I glance around. "There are a lot of people here."

He leans in so I can hear him. "Yeah. Let me put your coat in my room. C'mon."

He takes my hand and leads me out of the kitchen, through the living room, and down the hall to his bedroom, where the door is closed. I notice a group of girls taking notice of the fact that our hands are interlocked, and anxiety makes my heart rate pick up speed.

"Here." He holds his hand out for my coat and I slip it off and pass it to him. Lee drapes it on the back of the chair at his desk, then walks back to me. "C'mere shy pie. You didn't kiss me hello."

He pulls me into him, and our mouths meet. I'm not used to the fact that I can kiss this man whenever I want. The idea still feels foreign to me. But within a few seconds, all the noise from the party disappears and it's like it's just the two of us.

My nipples pebble in my bra and I grow wet between my legs. Before I know it, we're on the bed, making out.

That lasts for a few minutes before Lee pulls back. "Fuck, if we don't stop now, I'm gonna have you stripped and on my cock and then we're never leaving this room tonight."

I want to tell him I'm down with the idea, because the party makes me uncomfortable, but I know he needs to get back to the party. He is one of the hosts after all, not to mention a key member of the football team. I'm sure some of the players need to hear a good word from him in order to shake off the loss from today.

"You're right. Let's go back out to the party." My stomach flips with the thought of having to mingle with people I don't know for the rest of the night.

He stands and holds a hand out to help me up off the bed.

My back stiffens as soon as we're out of his bedroom. He never lets my hand go, but I see curious sets of eyes everywhere we go.

When Miles crosses the room, Lee lets go of my hand and places his on the small of my back. "Shayna, you remember Miles."

I nod. "Nice to see you again."

He holds my gaze. "Love RBG." He tips back his red solo cup.

"Where did you get the wig?" I ask.

I lift my hand to touch Miles's little dark curls and Lee slaps it away. "They're his own pubes he shaved off."

I backstep and Miles punches Lee in the stomach. They both laugh. "He's just kidding, but everyone thinks that." He picks up my hand, bends down, and places it on his head.

"Jesus, Miles, are you making another girl feel your pubes? I'm starting to get jealous." A cute redhead dressed as Barbie comes over to us.

Miles smiles and wraps his arm around her waist. "Only you get to touch the real ones."

"Ew. Gross. We gotta go." Lee takes my hand, pretending we're going to leave, but we stay in place.

"Shayna, this is McKenzie."

She puts out her hand, and we shake. Her smile is genuine and sweet. "Rumor was Burrows was hiding a girl."

Lee shakes his head.

"We're doing shots if you guys are in?" Miles nods toward the kitchen.

"Come on, Shayna, I say we pick a really girly one, snap a picture, and embarrass them all over Instagram." McKenzie locks her arm with mine and escorts me toward the kitchen. She weaves and squeezes by everyone without a care.

"Did the fuzzy nipple shot not teach you a lesson?" Miles screams over the partygoers.

McKenzie laughs and looks at me. "The guy literally is never embarrassed. So annoying at times."

The four of us sidle up to the hard alcohol area, cutting in front of people because it's their party. McKenzie pours the shots and we all raise them.

"To Shayna. Welcome to the group." She winks. Lee's arm tightens around my waist and McKenzie leans in close. "I have a good feeling about you."

I smile, hoping she's right, then I look at Lee, his Adam's apple bobbing when he downs his shot. I drink mine and we put our glasses on the table. Lee bends down and kisses me, tongue and all.

"Ew, PDA!" someone shouts.

Lee's mouth strips off of mine and I miss him immediately. "Get used to it!" he shouts back.

My face has to be flaming red from all the attention.

Miles comes up to me and holds my hands. "Number one, Shayna, you like yourself. Number two, you have to eat healthy. And number three, you've got to squeeze those buns."

I shake my head at him repeating Richard Simmons' catch phrase. He winks after he's done, and I know what he's saying. Who cares about everyone else in this party? As long as I like myself, that's all that matters. I've never felt welcomed so fast.

"Now, we're going to go dance and you're going to admire us from afar." McKenzie takes my arm and drags me into the family room, positioning us where the two guys can see us.

"How long have you been dating Miles?" I ask as we both shake our hips.

She looks over her shoulder at him. "About three months. He's a good guy. So is Lee. You're safe with him."

Before we even get through one song, the guys come behind us, and soon, Lee has me tucked into a corner with his tongue down my throat. Not that I'm complaining.

He rests his forehead on mine. "I gotta go to the bathroom. Be right back. Then I suggest we make an excuse and lock ourselves in the bedroom for the rest of the night."

"Sounds good." I nod. "I'll get a refill."

Lee disappears into the crowd. Rather than stand in the middle of the room by myself, I go into the kitchen to grab a drink.

The room is even more crowded than before, and there's a line for the spot on the counter where the makeshift bar is set up. Since I don't want beer, I decide to wait in the line. At the very least, I'm standing with a purpose rather than standing by myself like an idiot.

I'm waiting, sort of bopping my head to the beat, when I swear I hear my name.

"It's Shayna, dumbass, not Shayne," one of the guys in front of me in line says.

"Whatever. Who cares what her name is? Burrows hit that yet or what?" another guy asks. The guy in front of me is blocking me from seeing who either of them are.

"Doubt it. I'm sure if he had, he'd be gloating by now," another guy says.

"This whole thing was a stupid idea," the original guy who actually knew my name says.

"I don't know, man. I just saw them come out of his bedroom and it looked like something's going on with them."

I stiffen and look around to see if anyone else is eavesdropping or knows it's me they're talking about. Everyone else is busy in their own little pockets of people.

Some hooting and hollering from the other room distracts

me, but then one of them says something that makes my stomach bottom out.

"I knew our boy would win that bet. See, Siska? Never bet against Burrows. The guy could fuck any women he wants."

"It wasn't him I was betting on, it was the do-gooder. Damn it! I never thought she'd spread her legs for him. I was gonna be the one who finally got something Burrows couldn't. I hate losing a bet, man. Now I gotta explain to my dad where a thousand bucks went."

Tears spring to my eyes and I whip around and push my way through the crowd. People voice their complaints, but I need out of here before I cry.

A bet?

All I was to him was a bet? How did I not know that?

My vision is blurry as I ignore everyone I pass in the hallway, rushing to Lee's room to grab my coat and bag so I can leave. I send up a little prayer that I won't run into Lee on my way and God must be listening because I get out the door without seeing him.

I'm already mortified enough. The only thing that could make it worse would be to cause a scene and have everyone at the party know how stupid I am.

nine

. . .

Lee

I MAKE it back to the living room and glance around for Shayna, but I don't see her. She'd mentioned that she might she need a refill, so I make my way over to the kitchen but don't find her there either.

Huh.

I didn't see her in the hallway after I left the bathroom.

I spot Miles, Siska, and Bellamoore in the corner talking to a couple of chicks, so I approach them. "Any of you guys seen Shayna? I can't find her."

They all glance at each other and shake their heads.

"Haven't seen her, man," Miles says.

"Is that the girl dressed as RBG?" one of the girls asks.

"Yeah." I nod, hoping she's seen her.

"She was in front of me in line for the bar and I saw her bolt out of the room. She looked really upset."

My chest tightens. What the hell would've upset her?

I look at the guys and Siska has an "oh shit" expression.

"What happened?" I grind out between clenched teeth.

Miles raises both hands. "In all fairness, we had no idea she was within earshot."

"What happened?" I repeat, stepping forward.

"We were talking about the bet when we were making our drinks. If she was in line, it's possible she overheard us. So, did you do the deed?" Siska smiles, apparently not giving one shit about the fact I care for her. "I mean, I'm not asking for proof, but—"

"Fuck!" I roar. *Fuck, fuck, fuck.*

"Why do you care so much about her?" Bellamoore asks. "She's just a piece of ass, and if you nailed it, you get your truck back. No more walking for you."

My heart trips over a few beats when I think of how Shayna must've felt when she heard about the bet. I can only imagine the way these three were probably carrying on.

"I'm sorry, man," Miles says, but I'm already pushing my way out of the kitchen to see if she retreated to my room.

"Why are you sorry?" Siska asks. "I'm lost."

"Did you dipshits ever think maybe he fell for her and wasn't going to make you make good on the bet?" Miles says behind me. "He invited her here, didn't he?"

"To get some ass," Bellamoore says, obviously clueless. "To win the bet."

I get to my bedroom and whip open the door. Empty.

Damn it.

Yanking my phone from my back pocket, I dial her number, stepping into my room and closing the door.

No answer.

I try again, and this time, I'm sent to voicemail right away. Which means she did overhear and she's sending me there on purpose.

I press my fingers against the bridge of my nose and inhale deeply. It's okay. I can fix this. I'll just explain what happened, she'll understand, and we can move past it.

After I grab my jacket from my closet, I rush out of the

apartment without telling anyone. They've already done enough tonight. I'm pissed at them even if there is a voice in my brain that says it's my fault for not calling off the bet or telling her in the first place.

I have to make Shayna understand how much I've fallen for her.

It takes a while, but I finally figure out where Shayna lives and get someone to let me into her building. It helps that most people on campus are eager to please me and know I'm not some creep.

I make my way to her dorm room and knock on the door. No one answers, but I knock again because one of the girls downstairs told me she saw Shayna come in about a half hour before me.

After I knock again, there's shuffling behind the door. It opens halfway, revealing a red-rimmed-eyed Shayna.

"How did you find me?" Her face is blotchy too.

The sight threatens to bring up all the alcohol I've drank.

"I asked around. I need to talk to you."

"We have nothing to talk about." She moves to shut the door in my face, but I slap my hand on the wood, stopping it.

"Shayna... what you heard... it wasn't how it sounded."

She cocks out a hip. "So, you didn't make a bet with your friends that you could get me to sleep with you?"

I sigh, the nausea in my stomach growing.

"That's what I thought." She tries to close the door, but I stop it again.

"Yes, I made that stupid bet with them, but I never planned on going through with it. I just said yes to stop them from harassing me about you. Siska is an asshole and he was going to..." I can't continue because thinking of Siska trying to get her into bed disgusts me. "It was a stupid thing to do."

Her eyes narrow. "That's an understatement."

I grip her shoulders. "I'm sorry I hurt you. That's the last thing I ever wanted to do."

"Then why didn't you tell me about the bet before we slept together? You let me think this meant something to you. I feel like such an idiot."

I brush a tear that drops down her cheek. "It did mean something. *You* mean something. I really like you and I don't want to lose you."

She shakes her head. "That's not true. If you liked me, you would've been honest with me. Maybe not from the start, but certainly when we slept together. Do you have any idea what it felt like when I overheard your friends talking about me that way? Like I was a pity fuck. Like the only way you'd sleep with nerdy me was because they bet you?" Her voice is louder, and I see the ire in her eyes.

"I wanted to tell you. I did, I just… there never seemed to be a good time."

"Well, you don't have to worry about it anymore, because now that you're passing biology, you don't have to spend time with me again."

I let my hands drop from her shoulders. "Shayna… you don't mean that."

"I do. You should go." She steps back into her dorm room.

I put my foot out to stop the door from closing. "There has to be something I can do to make it up to you."

"Sometimes once something is broken, you can't fix it. Even if you glue all the pieces together, it'll never be the same as it once was." She inhales deeply, and tears gather again in her eyes. "You're not the person I thought you were, Lee. I'll never look at you the same way."

I inhale, but I feel as if there's no air. I step back, letting the door swing closed between us. When it thuds into place, I can't help but think how the sound is so final, as though it's a representation of the finality of Shayna's and my relationship.

With my head down so no one can see the unshed tears burning my eyes, I make my way out of the dorm.

I feel lost.

And angry.

And frustrated.

I fucked up and I have no one to blame but myself. That's the worst part.

I slump down onto a bench that lines the path, even though it's freezing out. Then I pull my phone from my coat pocket and pull up my brother's name. He should be finished with his game by now.

Kane answers on the second ring. "Hey."

"Hey."

"What's wrong?" Of course he can tell something is wrong with just one word. He's not my dad, but he's like a dad.

"I need a thousand dollars."

"Why?"

And so, I tell him everything that happened between Shayna and me.

In the end, he tells me that sometimes you have to learn to live with your mistakes and try not to repeat them, that sometimes there's no going back and fixing it.

I know he's right, but I vow that someday, somehow, I will make this up to Shayna.

————

Head over to **You Had Your Chance, Lee Burrows** for an **enemies to lovers, second chance romance** set eight years in the future when he's the **all-star quarterback** of the San Francisco Kingsmen and she's the new trainer on staff!

SCAN ME

about piper & rayne

Piper Rayne is a USA Today Bestselling Author duo who write "heartwarming humor with a side of sizzle" about families, whether that be blood or found. They both have e-readers full of one-clickable books, they're married to husbands who drive them to drink, and they're both chauffeurs to their kids. Most of all, they love hot heroes and quirky heroines who make them laugh, and they hope you do, too!

also by piper rayne

Kingsmen Football Stars

You had your chance, Lee Burrows

You can't kiss the Nanny, Brady Banks

Over my Brother's Dead Body, Chase Andrews

Hockey Hotties

My Lucky #13

The Trouble with #9

Faking it with #41

Sneaking around with #34

Second Shot with #76

Offside with #55

The Modern Love World

Charmed by the Bartender

Hooked by the Boxer

Mad about the Banker

The Single Dad's Club

Real Deal

Dirty Talker

Sexy Beast

Hollywood Hearts

Mister Mom

Animal Attraction

Domestic Bliss

Made in the USA
Middletown, DE
21 May 2023

31084070R00043